On Shabbat

On Shabbat

WRITTEN BY CATHY GOLDBERG FISHMAN
ILLUSTRATED BY MELANIE W. HALL

ATHENEUM BOOKS FOR YOUNG READERS
New York London Toronto Sydney Singapore

Atheneum Books for Young Readers
An imprint of Simon & Schuster Children's Publishing Division
1230 Avenue of the Americas
New York, New York 10020

Book design by Jim Hoover.

The text of this book is set in Novarese Medium.

The illustrations in this book are rendered in collagraph and mixed media.

Printed in Hong Kong

2 4 6 8 10 9 7 5 3 1

Library of Congress Cataloging-in-Publication Data
Fishman, Cathy.
On Shabbat / by Cathy Goldman Fishman ; illustrated by Melanie W. Hall
p.   cm.
Summary: Explains how a Jewish family celebrates the special day known as Shabbat each week.
ISBN 0-689-83894-8
1. Sabbath—Juvenile literature. [1. Sabbath.] I. Hall, Melanie W., ill. II. Title.
BM685.F54 2000
296.4'1—dc21   00-022584

To all the rabbis and their wives who helped bring Shabbat into my life:
Rabbi Maynard and Evelyn Hyman
Rabbi Jordan and Cynthia Parr
Rabbi Gary and Iris Atkins
Rabbis Alex and Amy Greenbaum

—C. G. F.

For my mother, Doris Goldfield Winsten,
I love you with all my heart.

—M. W. H.

*E*very Friday afternoon, all year long, we try to get home as quickly as we can. My father gives my mother a bunch of flowers and hands me two loaves of *challah*, bread fresh from the bakery. I know it is time to get ready for Shabbat, the most important Jewish holiday.

We put our schoolbooks in a closet. In go my mother's paints and my father's briefcase. My father says that Shabbat is a time to be happy. He says that we should put our problems in the closet, too, and bring out all of our questions. So I do.

on the seventh day God rested

"Why do we celebrate Shabbat every week?" I ask.

"Because," my father answers, "when God finished making the heavens, the earth, and everything on it, God rested. That was the seventh day, and God blessed that day and made it holy."

"That was the first Shabbat," my mother adds, "and God commanded us to celebrate Shabbat every week and make it different from every other day."

My grandmother says Shabbat is like a queen and
that every week we invite her to visit our house.
Everybody helps get ready for the Shabbat Queen.
    "We'll make the salad," my sisters sing out.
    "And I'll stir the soup," my father says.

While my grandmother and grandfather go to the Kabbalat Shabbat service at the synagogue, we set the table, fix the flowers, and set out small prayer books called *bentshers*.

We turn on the lights and put some coins in our Blue Box. We will send this *tzedakah* to the JNF so they can plant trees in Israel.

Just before sunset, my mother says, "It's time to make Shabbat."

I stand next to her as she lights the Shabbat candles. I circle my hands in the air over the flames and silently invite the Shabbat Queen to come into our house. I cover my eyes as we bless God, who commanded us to kindle the lights of Shabbat. When the blessing ends, everything seems different. It feels like the world has just taken a deep breath to relax and I know the Shabbat Queen has come to visit.

"*Shalom Aleikhem*, peace be with you," my grandmother and grandfather start singing when they come home from services. We all join in. Every week, after this song, I run to my mother and father to get their blessing. I love the feel of their hands on my head as they pray that God's spirit will shine on me. My brother and sisters get blessings, too.

Then my father smiles at my mother and reads from the *bentsher* that she is far above rubies. My mother smiles also and reads that my father is gracious, compassionate, and just. My sisters and I giggle together as we listen.

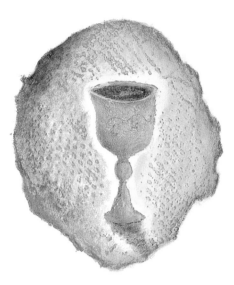

My grandfather likes to ask questions, too. This week he asks, "Who knows what the Friday night *kiddush* is about?"

"I know," one of my sisters answers. "It reminds us that this day is just as holy as the very first Shabbat."

"And we need to remember the Exodus from Egypt, when we didn't have to work as slaves anymore," I add.

"And it says that Shabbat is a present from God to me," my brother shouts.

"All of these answers are right," my grandfather states, and he sings with joy, chanting the *kiddush* in Hebrew and blessing God, Creator of the fruit of the vine.

Before dinner, we wash our hands and say *hamotzi* over the *challah*. We bless God, who brings forth bread from the earth. After dinner, we sing special Shabbat songs and thank God for the food, for our family, and for our friends. Every week Shabbat begins with candles, blessings, food, and song to make Shabbat different from every other day.

In the morning, we go to synagogue. I stand near my father and feel him gently sway back and forth as he prays, blessing God for creating light and darkness. Then I pray with him in Hebrew, "*Shema, Yisrael,* Hear, O Israel." I know all of the words.

I listen as the rabbi reads from the Torah and H*aftarah*. He chants a different part every week.

I hear the soft murmuring of the congregation as we pray and call God our Rock and our Shield. We pray that our lives will be full of peace and the words of Torah. We are in synagogue a long time. We say extra prayers to make Shabbat different from every other day.

"Shabbat shalom," we greet everyone as we head home for lunch.

"Is it still Shabbat?" my brother asks.

"Of course," my mother answers. "It will be Shabbat until we can see three stars in the sky."

My grandmother calls Shabbat a delight, a day that we all enjoy together.

"Let's play a game," my father says after we eat.

I choose team chess. My mother watches as my father and my brother play on one side and my sisters and I play on the other side. The winner gets to pick what to do next.

"It's nap time for me," my father says when his team wins.

"It's Torah study time for us," my mother says.

"Let's study about the flood and the rainbow God put in the sky," one of my sisters says.

"Let's study about Moses' staff and how it turned into a snake," my brother pleads.

"I want to learn about Moses' sister, Miriam, and the well that was named after her," I say.

"All right," my mother says. "We will study all of those miracles that we read about in the Torah. They are all special ways that God has helped us.

"It started in the beginning when God was creating the world. God worked for many days and when the sixth day was almost over, God still had lots to do."

"What was missing?" I ask.

"Well, I'll tell you," my mother replies. "The rabbis teach that at the twilight of the sixth day, in the very few seconds before that day was to end, God made the rainbow that appeared after the flood, Moses' staff, Miriam's Well, and many other miracles."

"I bet God was tired," my brother says.

"Yes," my mother says. "And when the seventh day began, God rested and made Shabbat different from every other day."

Shabbat afternoons are long and lazy, but all too soon I hear my brother.

"Come and look," he calls as he stands by the opened front door.

We gather around and look as he points to three stars in the dark evening sky.

"It's time to make H*avdalah*," my grandfather says. "It is time to end Shabbat and begin a new week."

"Here's everything we need," my father says. He holds a braided candle, a box filled with fragrant spices, and a cup of grape juice. My mother lights the candle and hands it to me. I hold it up high and try to count the wicks as they join together into one big flame.

My mother leads us as we sing the blessings that end Shabbat. We ask to be blessed with light and joy, and we bless God who created the fruit of the vine and sweet smelling spices. My grandmother shakes the spice box.

"Ahhh," she always sighs loudly after she breathes in the scent of the spices.

When I hold the spice box close to my nose and sniff deeply of the cloves and cinnamon, I feel stronger and ready to face a new week.

Then we bless God who made the lights of fire. We hold our curled fingers toward the flame of the H*avdalah* candle. I look at the light on my fingernails and at the shadow they make on the palm of my hand.

I look at the light and shadow on my hand as we bless God who separated light from darkness and Shabbat from the rest of the week.

When we drink the grape juice and put out the H*avdalah* candle, Shabbat is over.

"Good-bye, Shabbat Queen," my brother calls.

"*Shavua Tov*," my grandfather says to me. "Have a good week."

"*Shavua Tov*," I answer back.

I think that the busy weekday part of my life is like the *Havdalah* candle. All of my activities each day braid together to make one shining flame of my week. Now it is time to open the closet and take out our schoolbooks. Out come my mother's paints and my father's briefcase. Out come our problems, too, but I still get to ask questions.

"Can we make next Shabbat come faster?" I ask.

"No," my grandmother says with a laugh, "but we can start getting ready for it, right now."

We get out two new Shabbat candles and I put them in the holders. We will not light them yet, but each time I see them, I will feel Shabbat getting closer. The candles will remind me that soon it will be Friday afternoon and we will rush home as quickly as we can to make Shabbat different from every other day.

GLOSSARY

Bentshers (BEN churz): From the Yiddish word "bentsh" (bench) meaning to give a blessing. Small booklets containing the Grace after Meals and other prayers.

Challah (KHAL lah): A specially braided egg bread used for Jewish holiday meals. Two separate loaves are used for Shabbat because, when the children of Israel gathered manna in the wilderness, they gathered a double portion on Friday since there would be no manna the next day.

Haftarah (hahf tar RAH): A section chanted from the prophets following the chanting of the Torah.

Hamotzi (hah MO tzee): The blessing said over the *challah*, praising God for bringing forth bread from the earth.

Havdalah (hahv DAH lah): Hebrew for "separation." A ceremony that marks the transition between Shabbat and the rest of the week.

JNF (Jewish National Fund): An organization in Israel founded in 1901 to plant trees, conserve water and land, and turn desert wastelands into farming communities.

Kabbalat Shabbat (kah bah LAHT shah BAHT): A special service on Friday night to welcome Shabbat.

Kiddush (KIH dish): Hebrew for "sanctification," a prayer over the wine blessing God for creating the fruit of the vine. The Friday night kiddush also sanctifies the day of Shabbat, reminding us of the first Shabbat, the Exodus from Egypt, and that the Jewish people chose to accept the special gift of Shabbat.

Shabbat Queen (shah BAHT KWEEN): A symbolic reference to the joy of Shabbat.

Shabbat shalom (shah BAHT shah LOME): Hebrew for "Sabbath peace."

Shavua tov (shah VOO ah TOVE): Hebrew for "good week."

Shalom Aleikhem (shah LOME ah LEI khem): Hebrew for "peace be unto you," and is often used as a greeting. This is part of a hymn sung to welcome Shabbat angels of peace.

Shema, Yisrael (shuh MAH YIS ra ail): Hebrew for "Hear, Israel." This is part of a longer prayer proclaiming the oneness of God.

Tzedakah (tseh DUH kah): Money or other help given as a religious obligation to help the needy.

Torah (tor RAH): The Five Books of Moses. The word Torah also stands for all of the teachings of the oral and written traditions of Judaism. The example of Torah study used comes from Pirkei Avot, chapter 5, verse 8.